# Sing, Ping, Ting!

Written by Hatty Skinner

Collins

Hit it and bash it.

bang

3

Tap it with a thin rod.

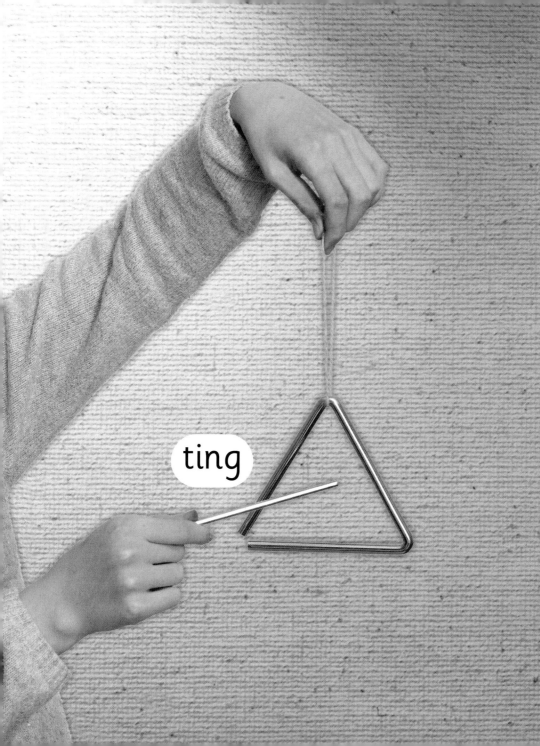

5

Sit and ping it.

ting ting ting

We huff and puff a jazz song.

I sing and they bop.

jig

Quick. Let us all sit.

/ng/

14

#  After reading

**Letters and Sounds:** Phase 3

**Word count:** 40

**Focus phonemes:** /j/ /w/ /z/ zz /qu/ /sh/ /th/ /ng/ /nk/

**Common exception words:** and, we, I, they, all

**Curriculum links:** Expressive arts and design

**Early learning goals:** Reading: read and understand simple sentences; use phonic knowledge to decode regular words and read them aloud accurately; read some common irregular words

## Developing fluency

- Your child may enjoy hearing you read the book.
- Demonstrate reading **bang** on page 3, and **ting** on page 5, in a tone that reflects the meaning of each word. Then take turns to read each left-hand page but join in together to read the labels on the right expressively.

## Phonic practice

- Focus on the words in which one sound is made up of two or more letters.
- Ask your child to sound out and blend the following:

    b/a/sh    p/i/ng    h/u/ff    s/o/ng    qu/i/ck    h/u/sh

- Say the words again. Can your child spell them aloud?
- Look at the "I spy sounds" pages (14–15) together. Take turns to find a word in the picture containing an /ng/ or /x/ sound. If necessary, prompt them to remember sound words by pointing to the triangle player and say: **Ting** – that's an /ng/ word. (e.g. *sing, ping, ting, king, song, sling, ringing phone, bang*; *box, fox, ox, saxophone, xylophone*)

## Extending vocabulary

- Ask your child to find the verbs in the book that are similar in meaning to:

    strike (*hit, bash, bang*)    knock (*tap*)    pluck (*ping*)    blow (*huff, puff*)    dance (*bop, jig*)